Dear Parent:
Your child's love of reading starts here!

Every child learns to read in a different way and at his or her own speed. Some go back and forth between reading levels and read favorite books again and again. Others read through each level in order. You can help your young reader improve and become more confident by encouraging his or her own interests and abilities. From books your child reads with you to the first books he or she reads alone, there are I Can Read Books for every stage of reading:

SHARED READING
Basic language, word repetition, and whimsical illustrations, ideal for sharing with your emergent reader

BEGINNING READING
Short sentences, familiar words, and simple concepts for children eager to read on their own

READING WITH HELP
Engaging stories, longer sentences, and language play for developing readers

READING ALONE
Complex plots, challenging vocabulary, and high-interest topics for the independent reader

ADVANCED READING
Short paragraphs, chapters, and exciting themes for the perfect bridge to chapter books

I Can Read Books have introduced children to the joy of reading since 1957. Featuring award-winning authors and illustrators and a fabulous cast of beloved characters, I Can Read Books set the standard for beginning readers.

A lifetime of discovery begins with the magical words "I Can Read!"

Visit www.icanread.com for information
on enriching your child's reading experience.

I Can Read Book® is a trademark of HarperCollins Publishers.

Man of Steel: Friends and Foes
Copyright © 2013 DC Comics.
SUPERMAN and all related characters and elements are trademarks of and © DC Comics.
(s13)

HARP29823

Printed in the United States of America. No part of this book may be used or reproduced in any manner whatsoever without written permission except in the case of brief quotations embodied in critical articles and reviews. For information address HarperCollins Children's Books, a division of HarperCollins Publishers, 10 East 53rd Street, New York, NY 10022.
www.icanread.com

Library of Congress catalog card number: 2012955957
ISBN 978-0-06-223595-4

Book design by John Sazaklis

13 14 15 16 17 LP/WOR 10 9 8 7 6 5 4 3 2

❖

First Edition

I Can Read!™
READING 2 WITH HELP

MAN OF STEEL™

Friends and Foes

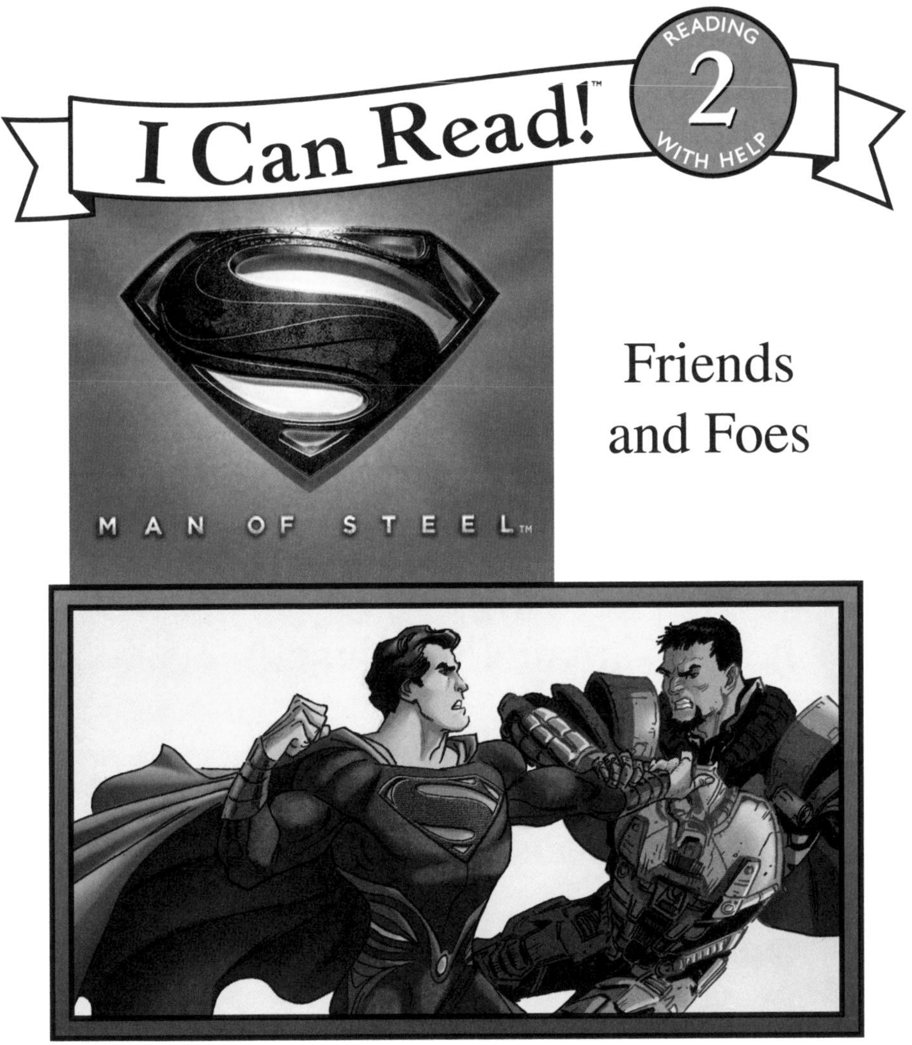

Adapted by Lucy Rosen
Pictures by Steven E. Gordon
Colors by Eric A. Gordon
Cover art by Jeremy Roberts

INSPIRED BY THE FILM MAN OF STEEL
SCREENPLAY BY DAVID S. GOYER
STORY BY DAVID S. GOYER AND CHRISTOPHER NOLAN
SUPERMAN CREATED BY JERRY SIEGEL AND JOE SHUSTER

HARPER
An Imprint of HarperCollins*Publishers*

Meet Clark Kent.

He lives on Earth but

he is from another planet!

On the outside,

he might look like a regular guy.

But Clark has a secret past.

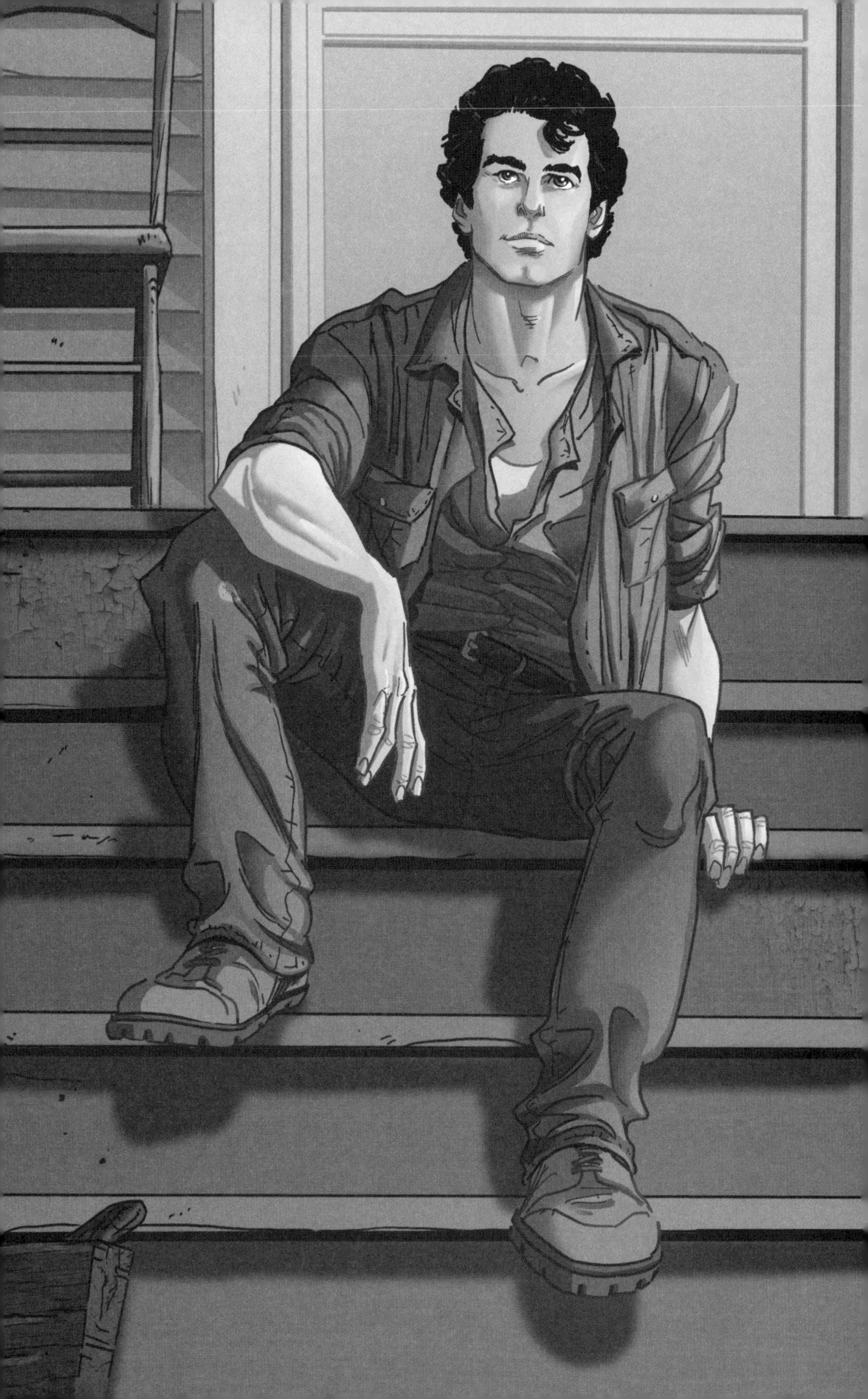

Clark was born on a planet
known as Krypton,
far in outer space.
His real name is Kal-El.
His parents, Jor-El and Lara,
loved him very much.

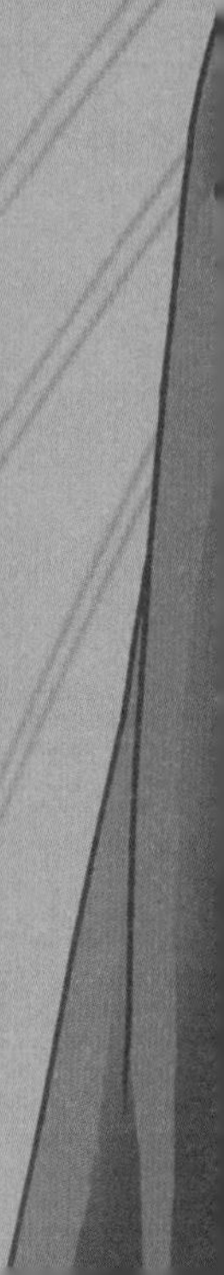

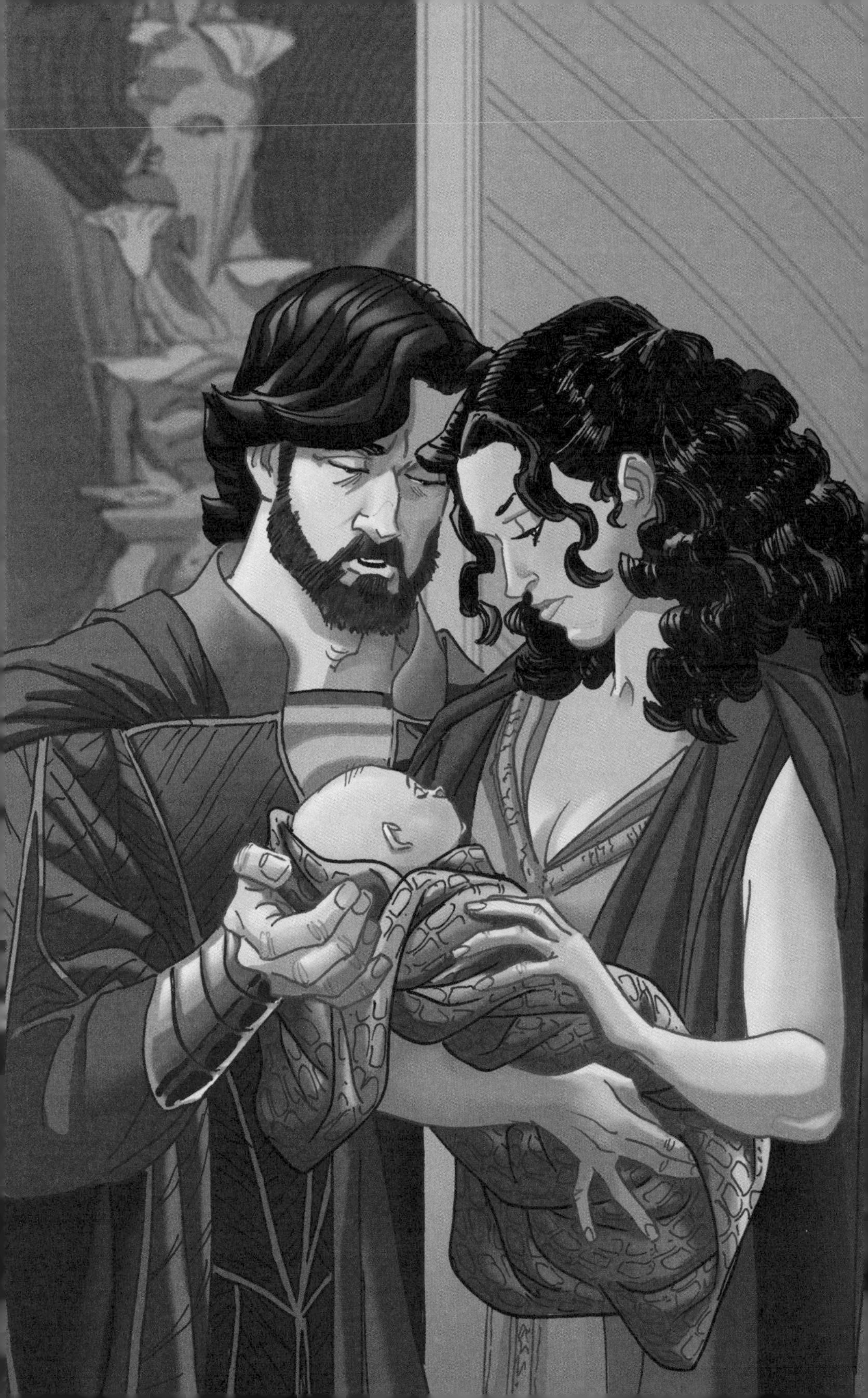

Kal-El and his family
lived in a beautiful home
called the House of El.
They had two robot servants
named Kelex and Kelor.

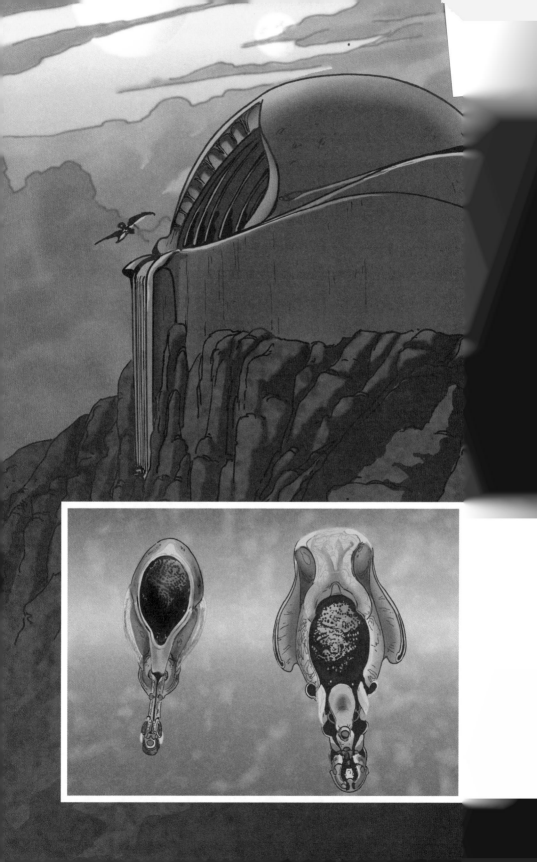

Jor-El was a scientist.

He found out that Krypton

was going to explode.

Jor-El went to the ruling council

with this discovery.

They did not believe him.

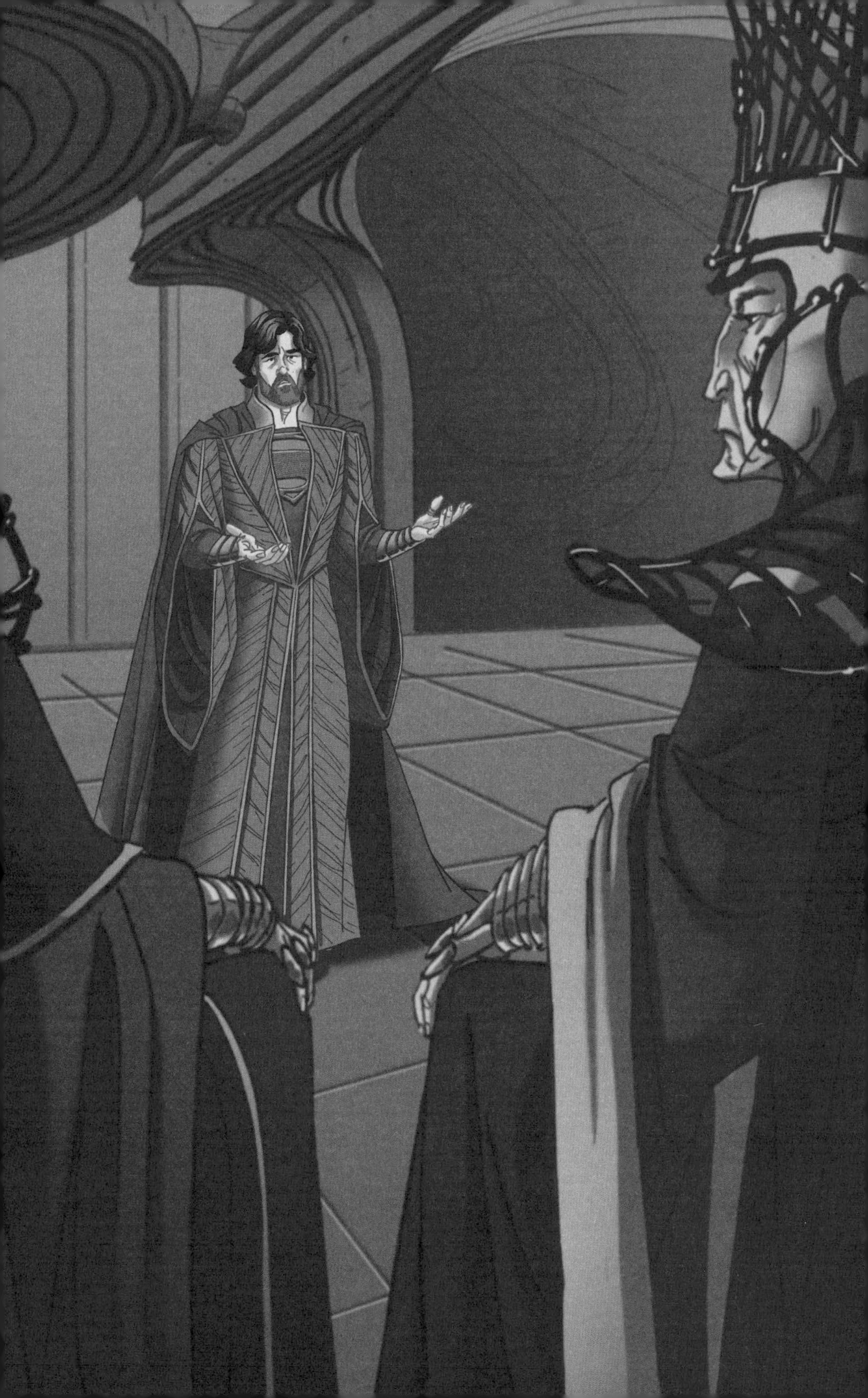

Lara and Jor-El wanted

to save their son.

To grow up safely, Kal-El

would have to leave Krypton.

Lara put the baby

in a small spacecraft.

Jor-El said to his son,

"You are our last hope."

The ship launched into space.

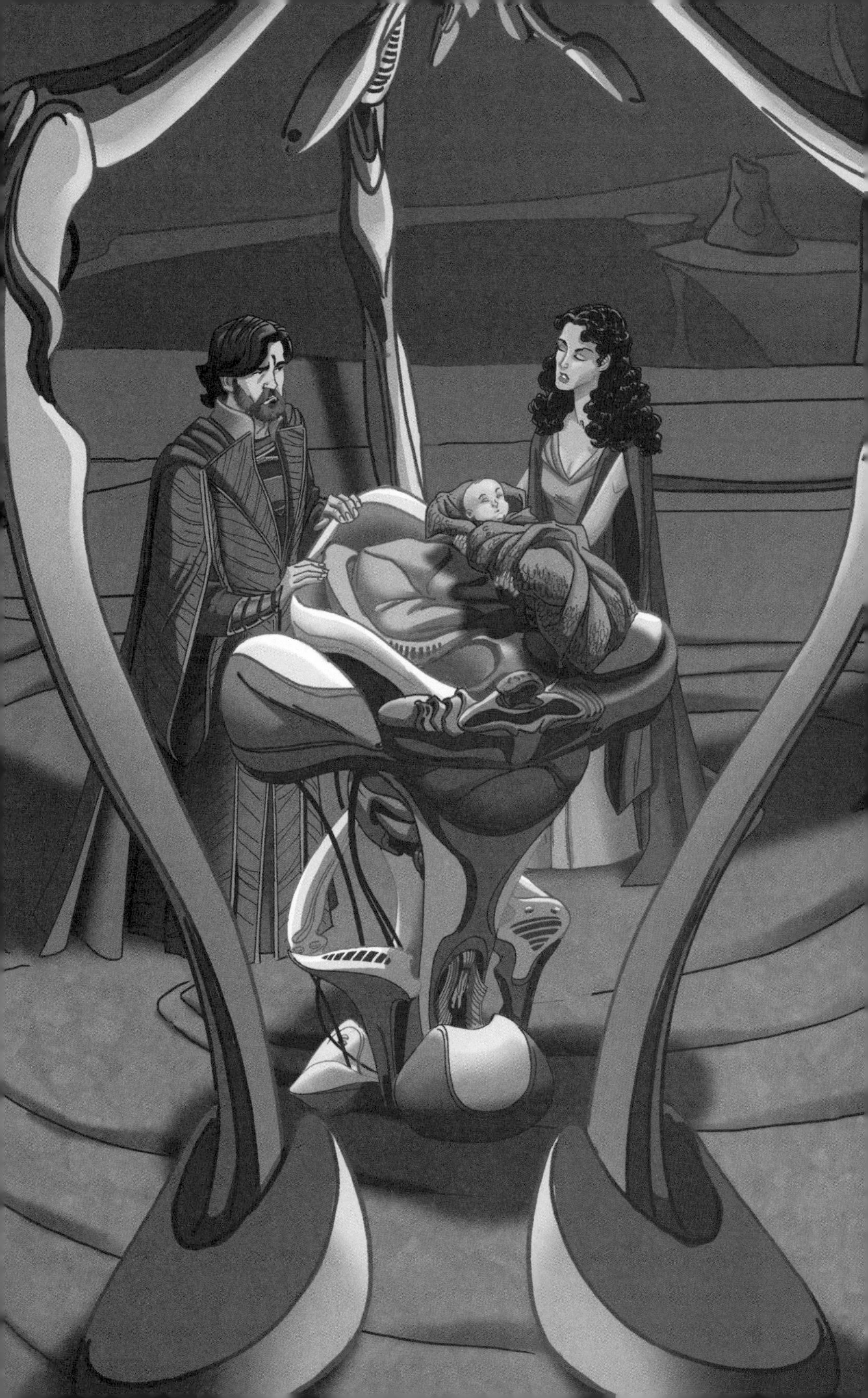

Kal-El's spacecraft

landed on Earth with a crash.

Martha and Jonathan Kent

found it near their farm.

They discovered the baby inside.

Martha and Jonathan

gave Kal-El a new name—

Clark Kent—

and became his Earth family.

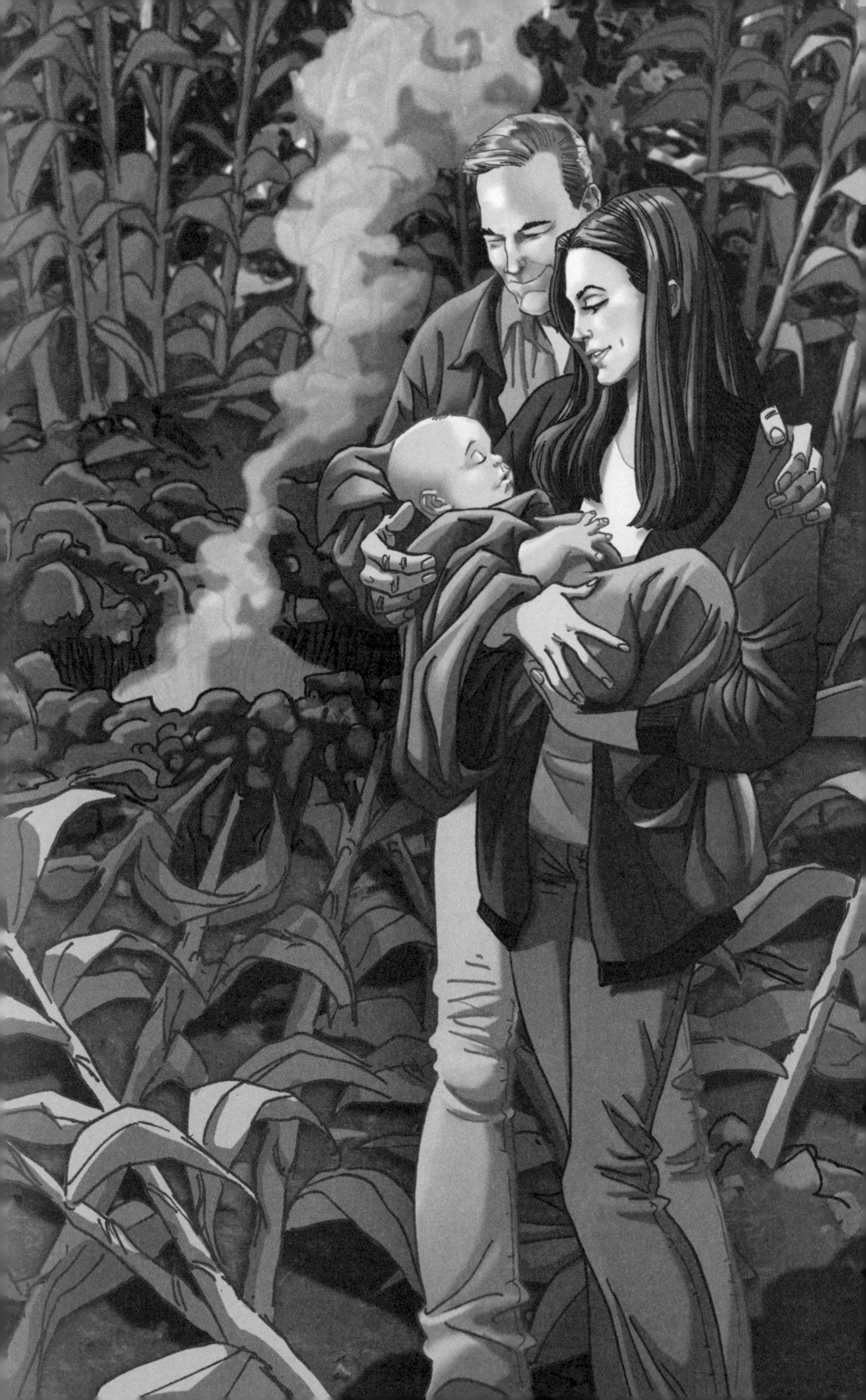

Clark grew up like any other boy.

He went to school.

But Clark was very different.

He had special powers!

He was super-fast, super-strong,

and he could fly!

Clark kept his superpowers secret.

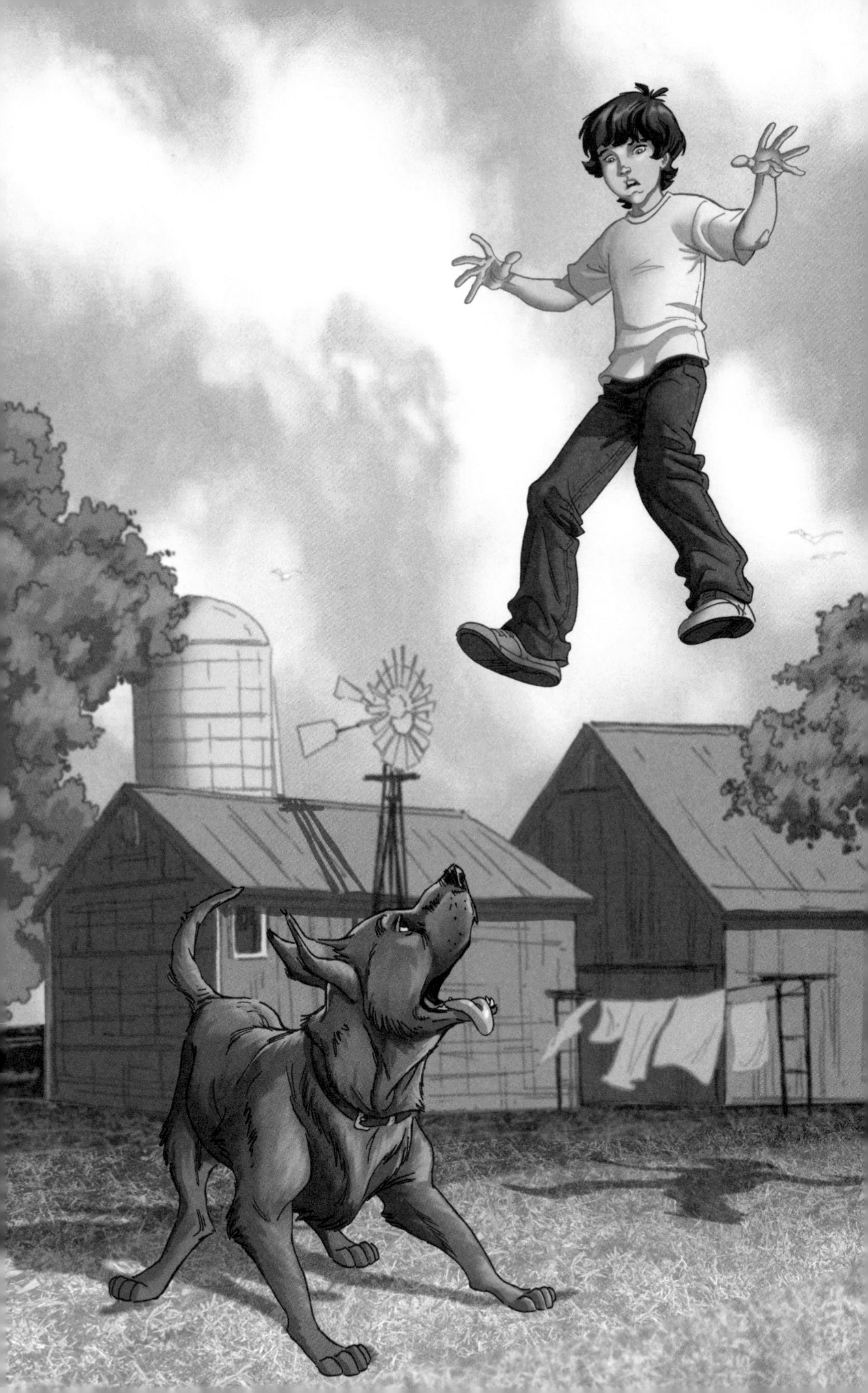

Clark had trouble at school

with bullies like Pete Ross.

He teased Clark

and called him names.

Luckily, Clark had a kind and

loyal friend named Lana Lang.

She stood by his side.

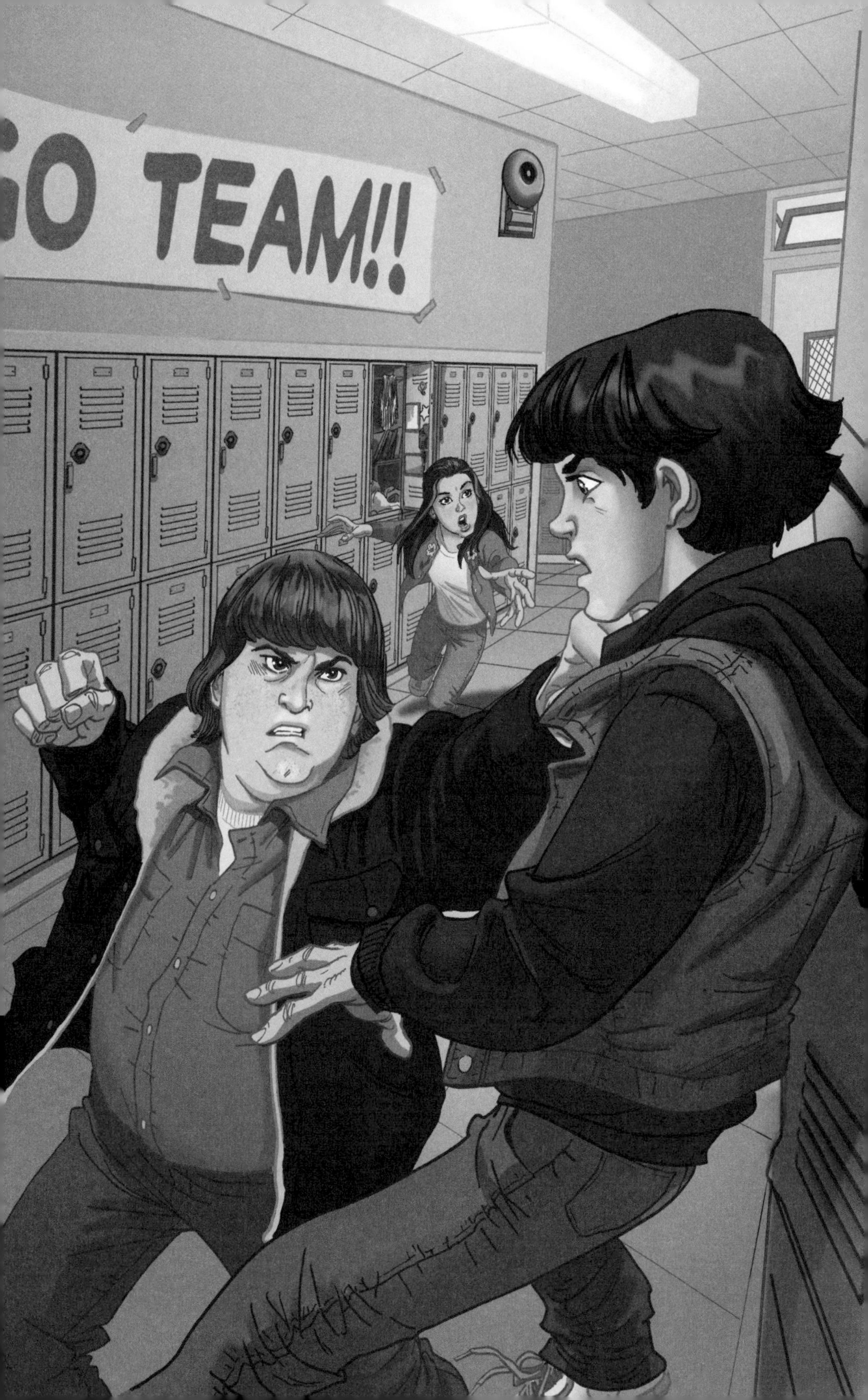
GO TEAM!!

Today, Clark Kent
is a grown-up.
He travels the world
and does good deeds.
He uses his superpowers
to save people.

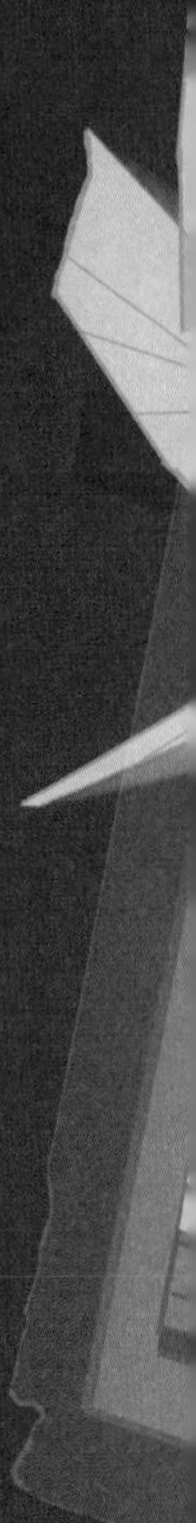

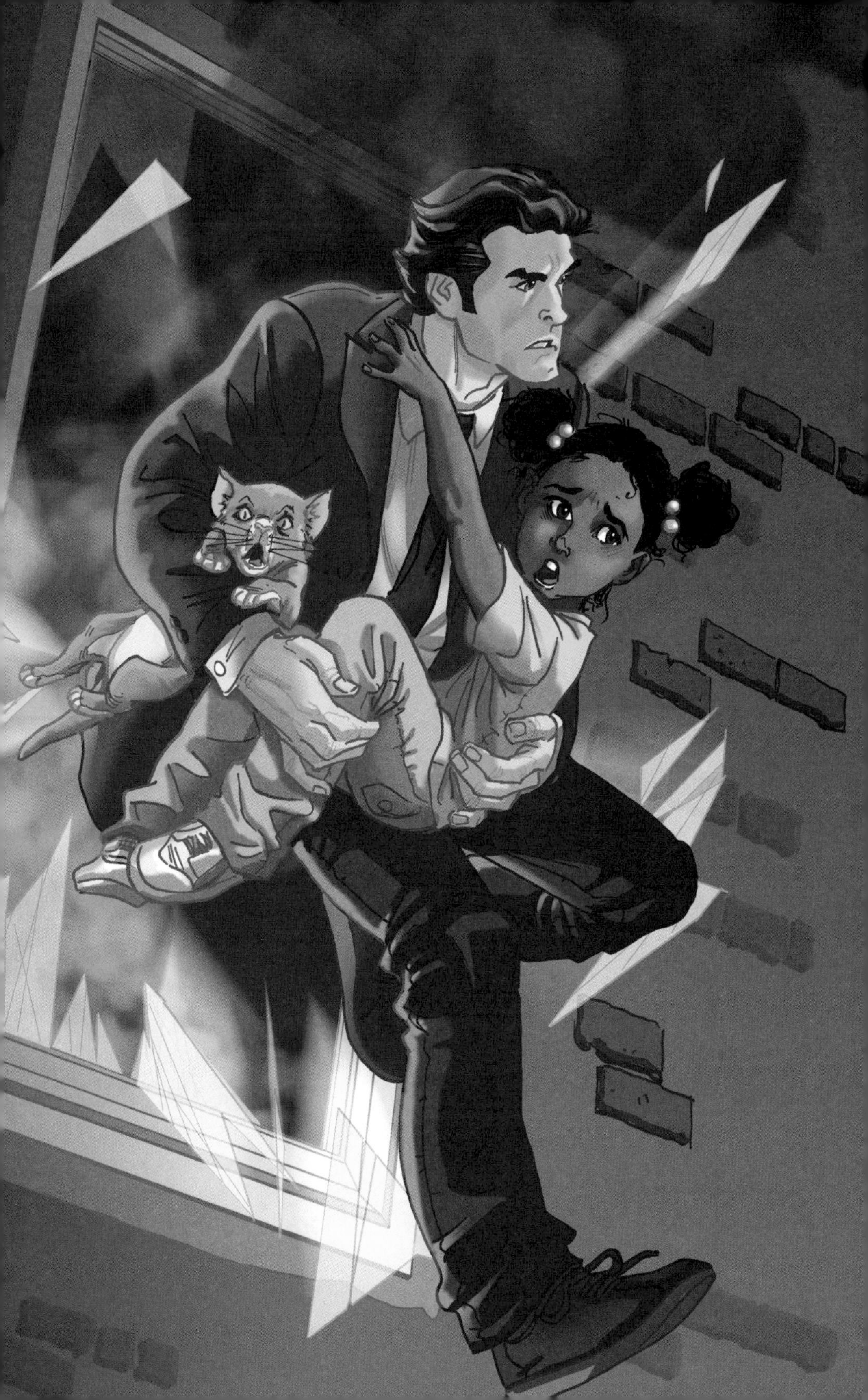

One day,

an alien ship arrives from space.

On board is General Zod,

a criminal from Krypton!

He lands in Smallville

and attacks Earth.

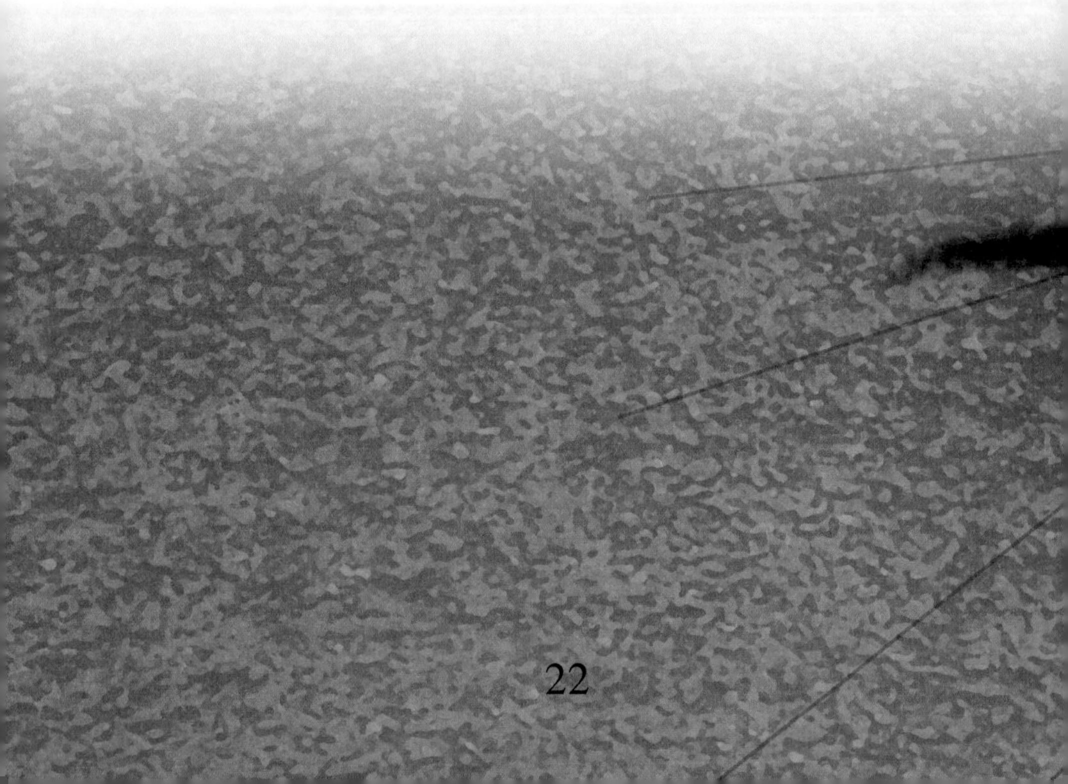

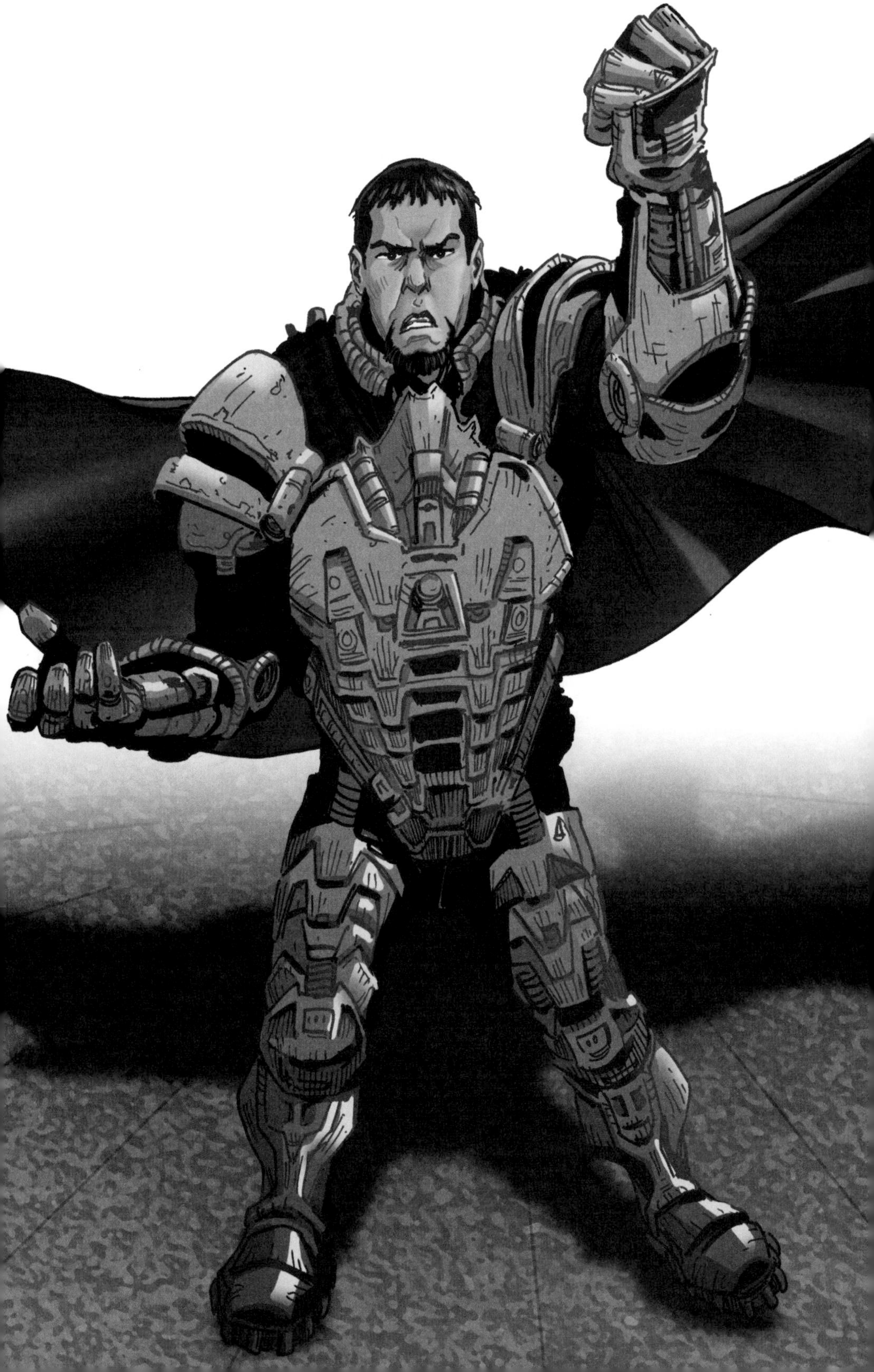

With General Zod

are two other criminals

named Faora and Nam-Ek.

They are fierce warriors

bent on destruction.

They will stop at nothing

to rule Earth with Zod.

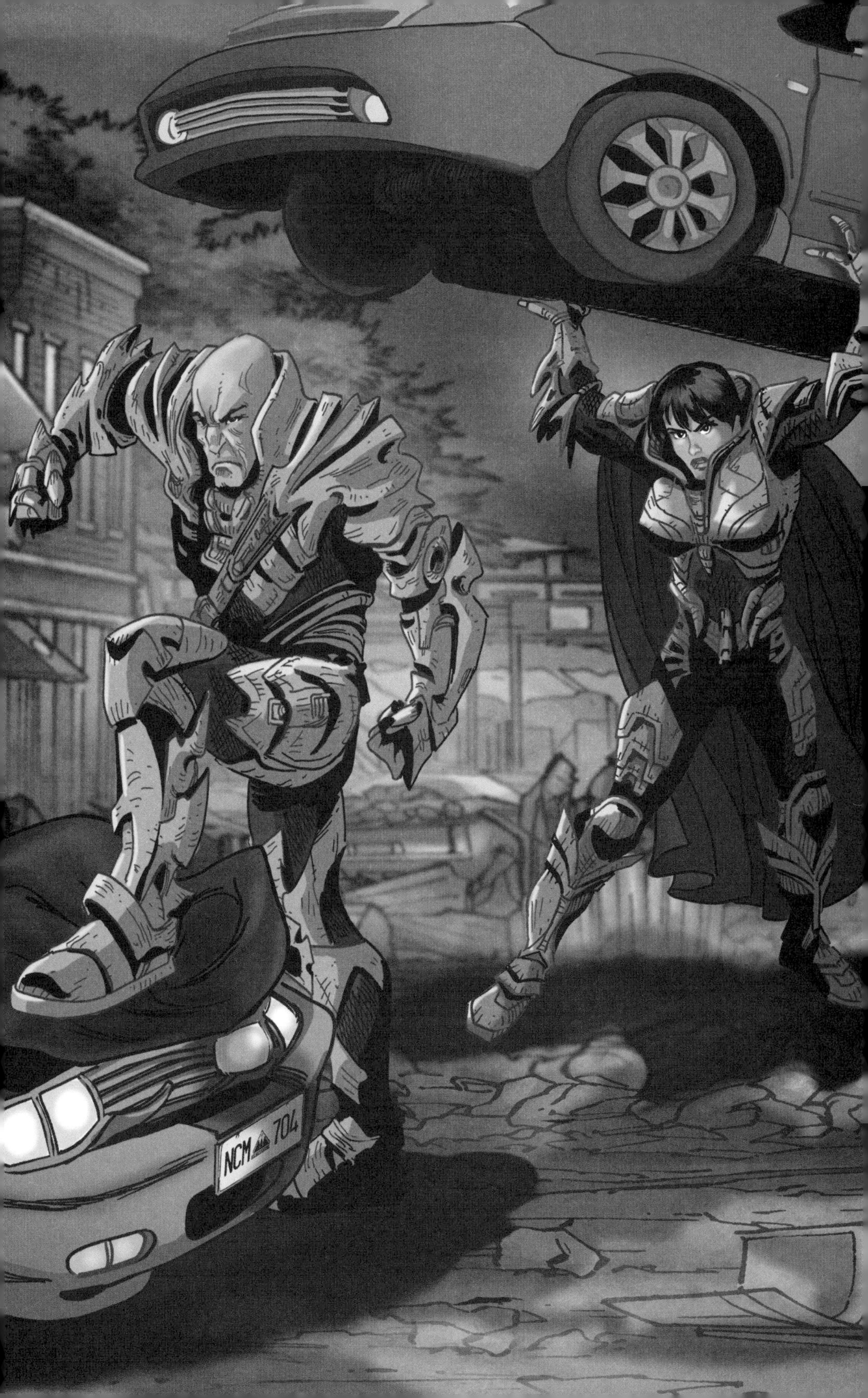
NCM 704

Clark knows that he is the only one
who can defeat this alien menace.
He will not let these evil villains
destroy his new home.
It is time to use his powers
to stop the bad guys!

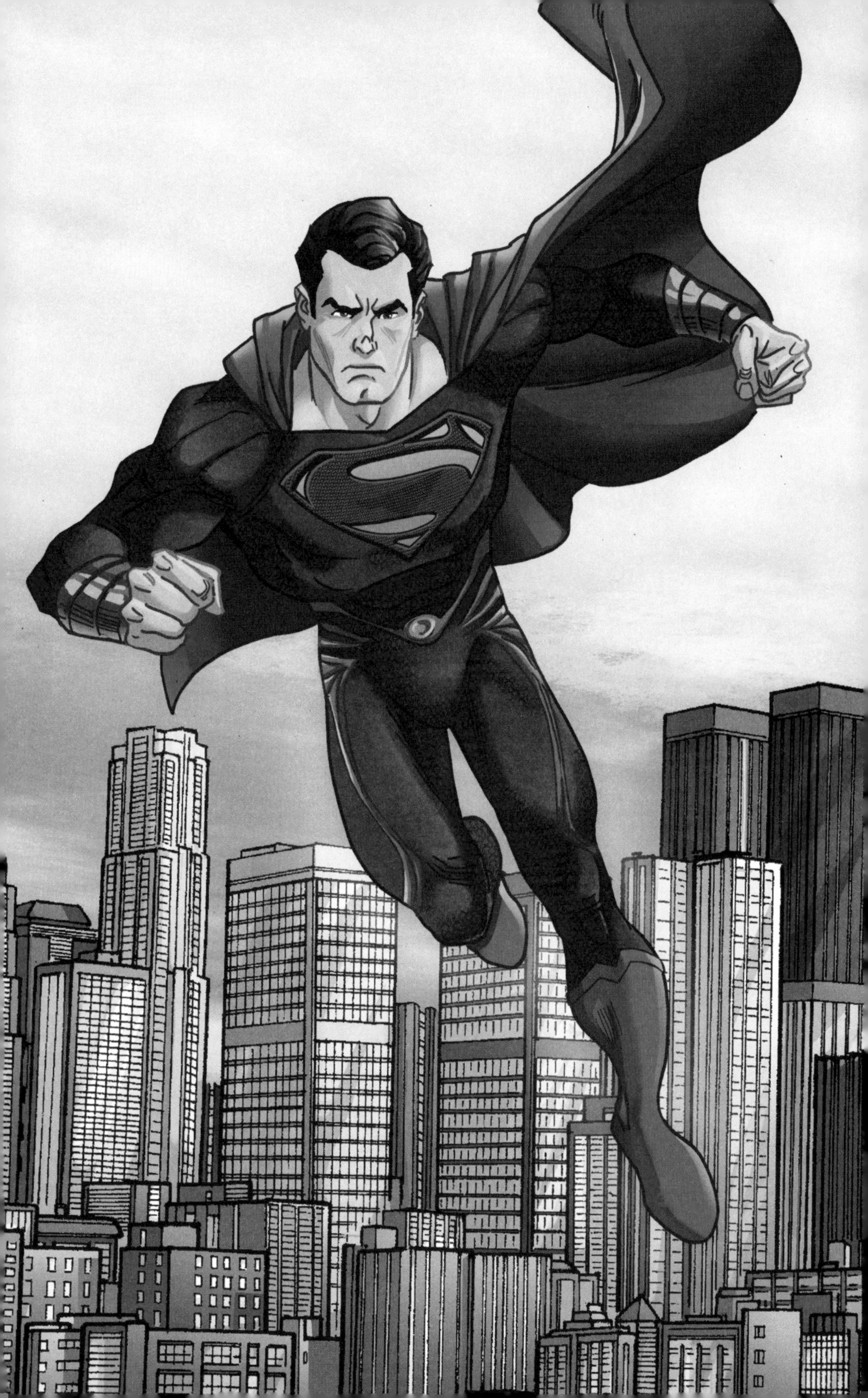

Clark's new foes have

superpowers just like he does.

The battle is fierce,

but Clark wins.

General Zod and his helpers

retreat back to outer space.

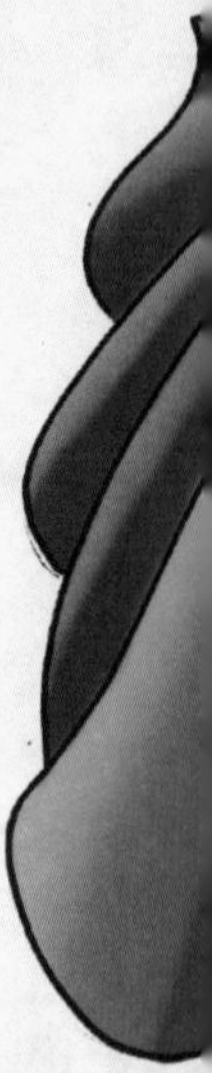

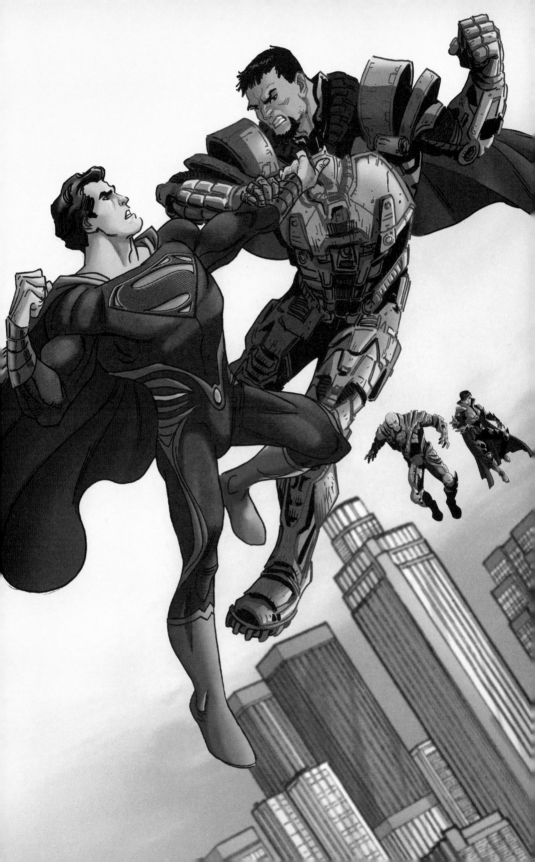

Perry White is the editor

of the *Daily Planet* newspaper.

Lois Lane is its ace reporter.

She doesn't know who the hero is,

but she gives him a name.

She calls him Superman!

Perry prints her story

on the front page.

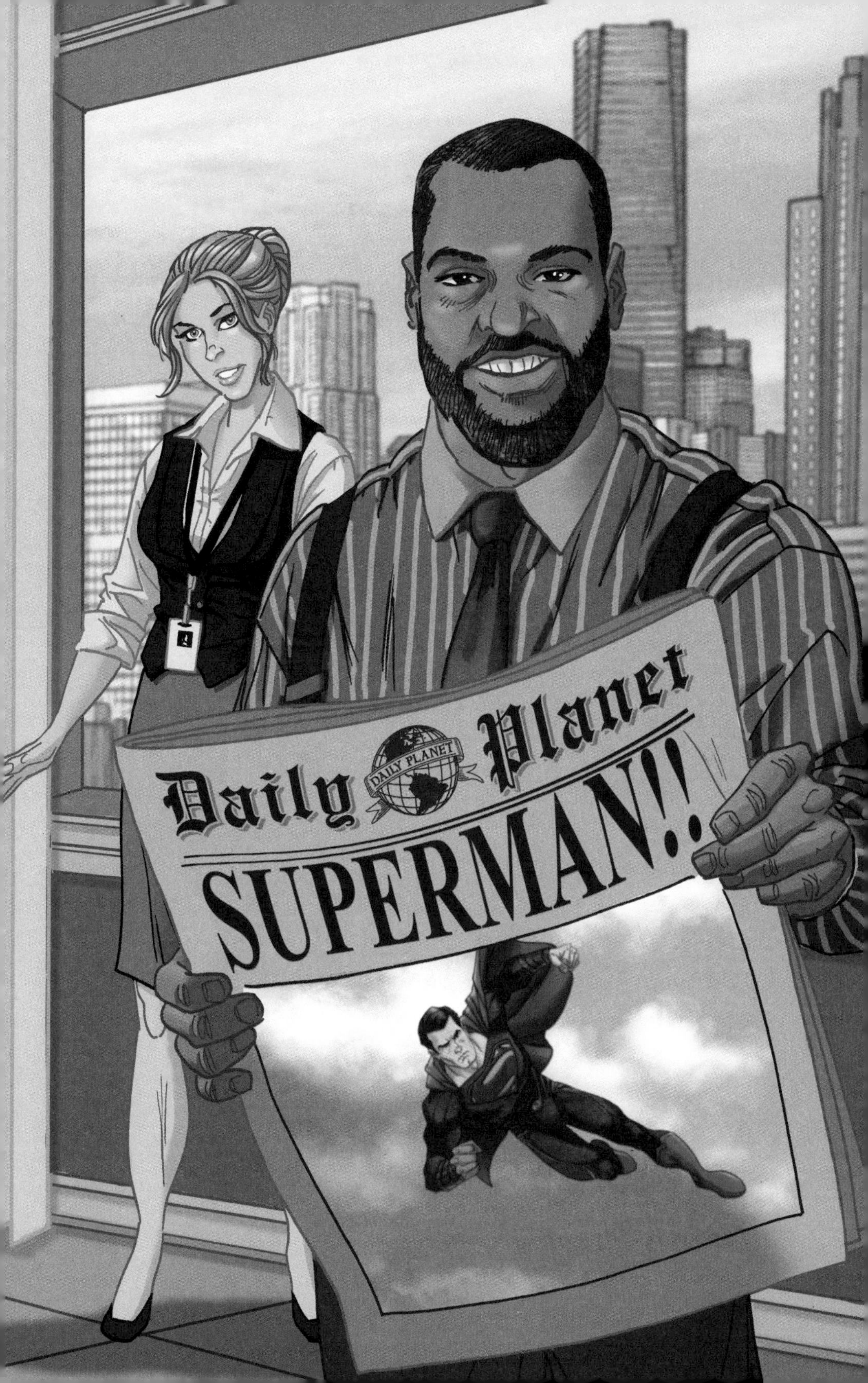
Daily Planet
DAILY PLANET
SUPERMAN!!

Clark Kent is Superman.
He will do everything he can
to keep Earth safe
from Zod and other villains.
He is the Man of Steel!

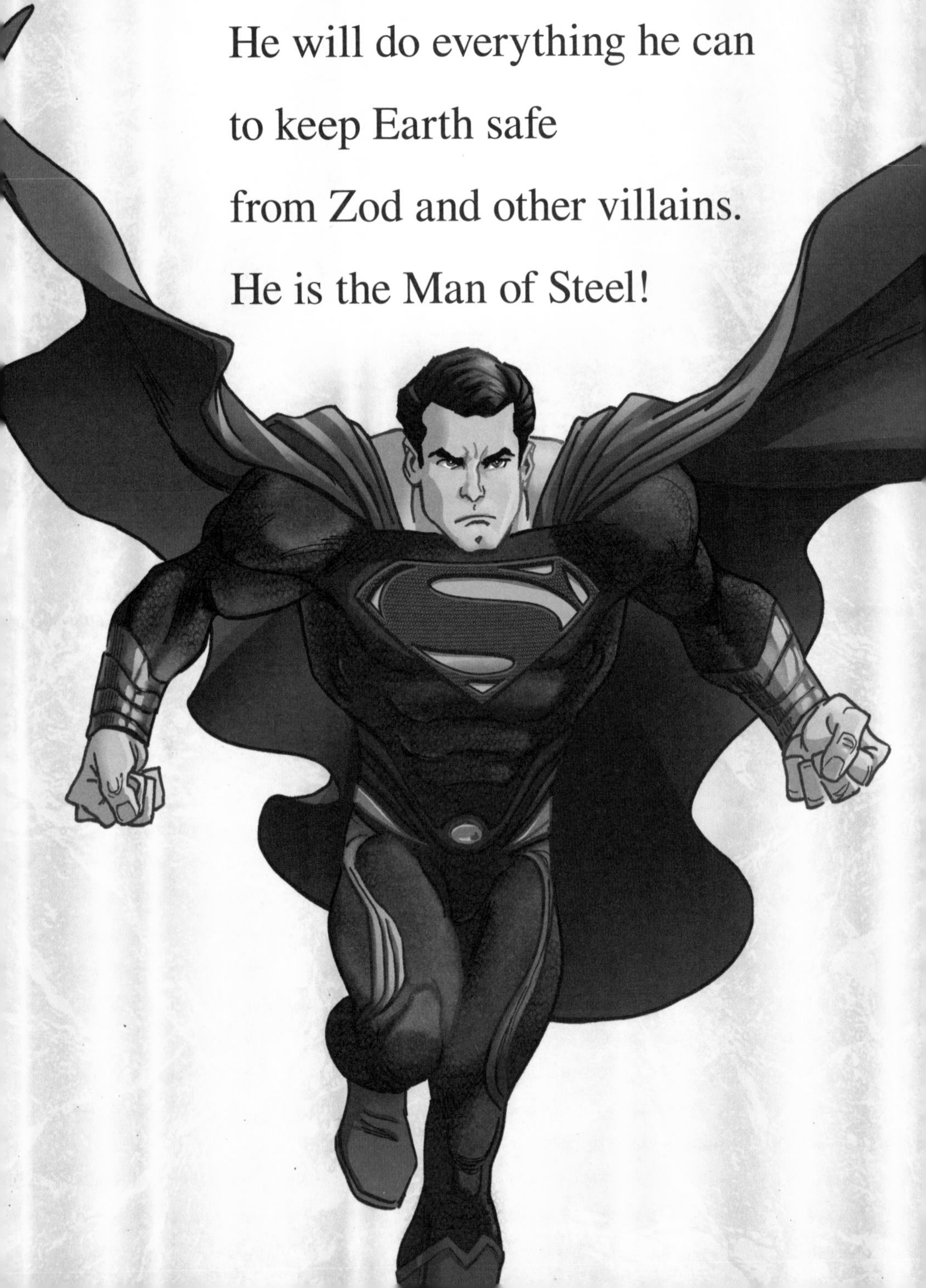